Town and Country Mice

RAVETTE PUBLISHING

RSPCA name and logo and Perfect Pets name are trademarks
of RSPCA used by Ravette Publishing Ltd under licence from
RSPCA Trading Ltd.

RSPCA Trading Ltd (which pays all its taxable profits to RSPCA,
Registered charity no. 219099) will receive a minimum of £2,500
from the sale of this product line.

© 2002 RSPCA
Perfect Pets ® RSPCA registered trademark
www.rspcaperfectpets.com
www.licensingbydesign.co.uk

First published by Ravette Publishing 2005
Illustrated by Adam Pescott
Written by Gordon Volke

Printed and bound in India for
Ravette Publishing Limited,
Unit 3, Tristar Centre,
Star Road, Partridge Green,
West Sussex RH13 8RA

ISBN: 1 84161 171 9

Chalk was a little white mouse. His brother, Cheese, was brown. They were always together and slept on top of each other in a pile!

The mice were for sale in Homefield pet shop. The owner, Mr Marshall, put them on display in the window when the sun was not too hot.

Molly Kingston loved the lively little creatures. So she saved up her pocket money and, one day, she had enough to visit the pet shop with her mum.

Molly bought Chalk as a pet.
"I'd love Cheese as well," she sighed,
"but I don't have enough money to buy
them both at the same time."

The little girl took Chalk home and put him in a nice new cage. She thought he would be happy, but he wasn't!
"I want to be with Cheese," he murmured, sadly.

Back in Homefield pet shop, Cheese felt just the same. So, when Mr Marshall left his cage open by mistake, he escaped to find his brother.

Cheese scurried through the back streets and alleyways of the town.

"No sign of Chalk," he sighed, nibbling some scraps from a dustbin.

Molly lived in a country cottage just outside Homefield.
"A look round the garden will cheer you up, Chalk!" she chuckled.
But her mouse escaped too!

Ignoring Molly's cries, Chalk ran off to find Cheese. He scampered down a country lane, stopping only to drink from the puddles.

A road ran from Homefield to Molly's cottage. Cheese made his way along one side, heading out from the town to the country.

Meanwhile, his brother Chalk headed back from the country to the town on the other side of the road.
They passed each other without knowing!

Being on their own, both the little mice were in danger. A kestrel spotted Cheese and the silent bird of prey swooped down to catch his dinner.

Luckily, Molly saw what was happening and rescued the mouse.

"You're not Chalk!" she gasped in amazement. "You're his brother, Cheese!"

A cat chased Chalk right into Homefield
town centre. Mr Marshall helped out this
time.

"Go away, puss!" he called, clapping his
hands and gently shooing off the cat.

The pet shop owner expected to pick up his escaped mouse.

"I don't believe it!" he exclaimed. "This isn't Cheese. It's Chalk!"

Both the mice looked thin and tired, so their new owners took them to the local vet for a check-up.

Molly and Mr Marshall met in the vet's waiting room.

"You've got Chalk!" gasped the little girl.

"And you have Cheese!" exclaimed the shopkeeper.

The vet, Mr Charles, examined the runaway mice.

"They're both fine!" he said. "But they mustn't be parted again. They need to be with each other!"

On their way home, Molly and Mr Marshall
called at the RSPCA Animal Rescue Centre.

"What an amazing story!" said Karen, the
animal care assistant.

"We can put it in 'Animal Action', our
children's magazine."

A few days later, Mr Marshall let Molly spend the rest of her money buying Cheese as well.

"He comes with a special free gift," chuckled the kind shopkeeper.

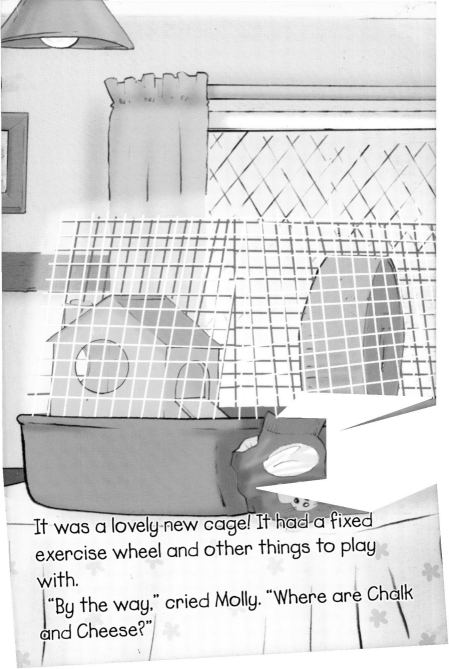

It was a lovely new cage! It had a fixed
exercise wheel and other things to play
with.

"By the way," cried Molly. "Where are Chalk
and Cheese?"

The two cheeky mice had already gone to bed! They were fast asleep in their little bed, lying in a pile on top of each other, as usual.

Taking on a pet is a big decision
– they can be expensive and
need lots of care.

Every year, lots of pets are dumped
when their owners find they can't cope.

Only the lucky ones are rescued and
rehomed by the RSPCA.

If you love animals and would like to join
the Animal Action Club and receive
their great magazine Animal Action,
call 0870 333 5999
for further details.

Other **Perfect Pets** titles available . . .

Story Books @ £2.99 each	ISBN
Bob the Old English Sheepdog (Please Take Me Home)	1 84161 164 6
Cassie the Posh Cat (Staying in Shape)	1 84161 169 7
Hamish the Hamster (Star of the Show)	1 84161 172 7
Lucky the Cat (Be Patient With Me)	1 84161 165 4
Rosie the Rabbit (Will You Be My Friend?)	1 84161 167 0
Ruff the Lively Rascal (A Good Dog is a Safe Dog)	1 84161 170 0
Scraps the Labrador Puppy (A Friend For Life)	1 84161 166 2
Activity Book @ £2.99	1 84161 174 3

TO ORDER . . .

The **Perfect Pets** books are available from all good bookshops, or direct from the publisher at the following address:

Ravette Publishing Ltd
Unit 3, Tristar Centre, Star Road, Partridge Green,
West Sussex RH13 8RA (Tel: 01403 711443)

Prices and availability are subject to change without notice. Please send a cheque in £ sterling made payable to 'Ravette Publishing' for the cover price + 50p per copy UK postage and packing.